The North Wind and the Sun

For Aurélie and also for all children,
young and old.

OXFORD
UNIVERSITY PRESS

Great Clarendon Street, Oxford OX2 6DP

Oxford University Press is a department of the University of Oxford.
It furthers the University's objective of excellence in research, scholarship,
and education by publishing worldwide in

Oxford   New York

Auckland   Cape Town   Dar es Salaam   Hong Kong   Karachi
Kuala Lumpur   Madrid   Melbourne   Mexico City   Nairobi
New Delhi   Shanghai   Taipei   Toronto

With offices in
Argentina   Austria   Brazil   Chile   Czech Republic   France   Greece
Guatemala   Hungary   Italy   Japan   Poland   Portugal   Singapore
South Korea   Switzerland   Thailand   Turkey   Ukraine   Vietnam

Oxford is a registered trade mark of Oxford University Press
in the UK and in certain other countries

© Brian Wildsmith 1964

The moral rights of the author/illustrator have been asserted

Database right Oxford University Press (maker)

First published 1964
First published in paperback 1986
Reissued in paperback 1999
This new edition first published in paperback 2007

British Library Cataloguing in Publication Data
Data available

ISBN 978-0-19-272707-7 (paperback)

1 3 5 7 9 10 8 6 4 2

Printed in China

Brian Wildsmith

The North Wind and the Sun

OXFORD
UNIVERSITY PRESS

One morning the North Wind and the Sun

saw a horseman
wearing a new cloak.

'That young man looks very pleased with his new cloak,' said the North Wind. 'But I could easily *blow it off his back* if I wanted to.' 'I don't think you could,' said the Sun. 'But let us both try to do it. You can try first.'

The North Wind began to

blow and *blow* and *blow*.

People
had to
chase
after
their
hats.

Leaves were blown from the trees.

All the animals
were frightened.

The ships in the harbour were sunk.

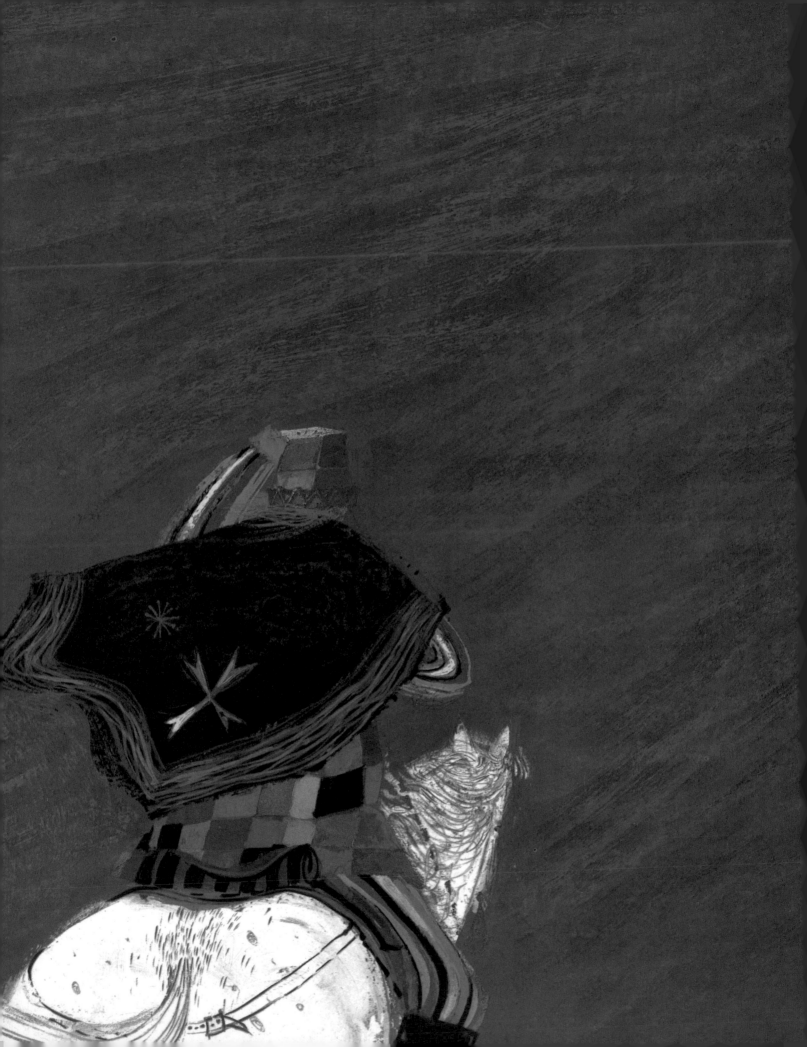

The North Wind
blew *with all
his might*,
but it was no use,
for the horseman just
pulled his cloak more
tightly around him.

'My turn now,'
cried the Sun.

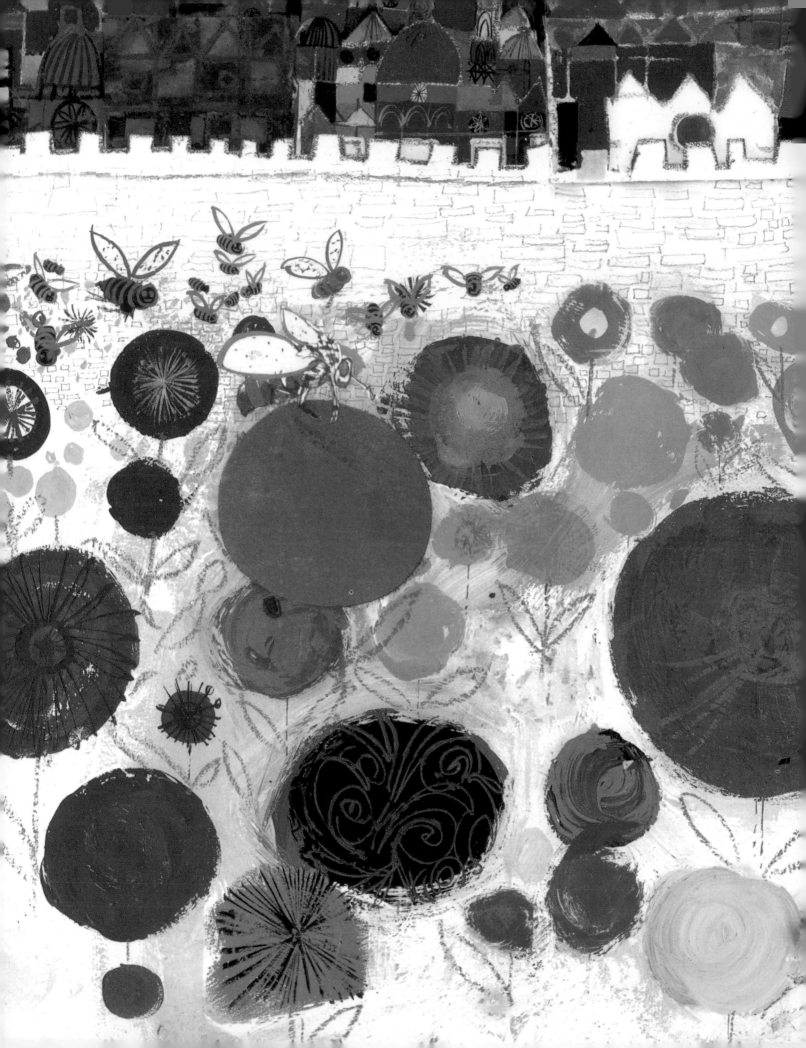

And as he gave
out his gentle heat,
insects hummed
and flowers opened.

The birds began to sing.

The animals lay down to sleep.

And the people came out to gossip.

The horseman
began to feel
very hot,
and when he came
to a river he took off
his clothes and went
in for a swim.

So the Sun was able to *achieve by warmth and gentleness* what the North Wind in all his *strength and fury* could not do.